by **Nanette Kalis**

***Illustrated by* Drew Rose**

The Moon Colony
by Nanette Kalis

Illustrations by Drew Rose

Fiction Reviewer
Charles E. Martin, Ph.D.
Professor of Early Childhood and Middle Grades Education
Georgia College & State University

Design, Production, and Art Buying by
Inkwell Publishing Solutions, Inc., New York City
Cover Design by
Inkwell Publishing Solutions, Inc., New York City

ISBN: 0-7367-1869-9
Copyright © Zaner-Bloser, Inc.

All rights reserved. No part of this book may be reproduced or transmitted in any form or by any means, electronic or mechanical, including photocopying, recording, or by any information storage and retrieval system, without permission in writing from the Publisher.
Zaner-Bloser, Inc., P.O. Box 16764, Columbus, Ohio 43216-6764, 1-800-421-3018

Printed in China

03 04 05 06 07 (321) 5 4 3 2 1

Table of Contents

Chapter One

"Here's to Sam, Sherra, and Adam—may they have the adventure of a lifetime!"

I rolled my eyes as my uncle Ronnie raised his glass high and made the toast to my parents and me. About 40 people were standing in our living room, clapping and shouting, "Here, here!" They were having a good time. It was a party, after all. But I wasn't having any fun. I was sitting on the end of the couch with my chin propped in my hand, staring at nothing in particular. The only thought in my mind was this:

Today is my last day on Earth.

You're probably thinking that I'm going to die or something. But no, it's nothing like that. Today is my last day on Earth because tomorrow morning, bright and early, I'm going to the moon. My parents work for the Global Outer Space Council, or GOSC for short. My mom's an engineer and my dad's a geologist. And lucky me, we were one of only five families in the world who were chosen to live in the new Moon Colony.

There'll be other people there—technicians and such—but only five real families.

"Adam?" someone called.

I looked up to see my neighbor, Ms. Perzana, standing in front of me. Her face showed concern. "Are you all right?" she asked.

I shrugged. "Sure. I'm dandy."

"Well then, why aren't you outside with your friends?"

Why don't you mind your own business? I thought. Then I felt bad because Ms. Perzana has always been nice to me. Last summer, I was playing laser tag with my friends and I broke her window and she didn't get mad. She just said, "Cut my grass and we'll call it even." I didn't mind because she has one of those new riding mowers made of fluid metal—they flow like mercury, curving around trees, then straightening out again.

I was about to tell Ms. Perzana that I was tired and just wanted to sit quietly for a while. Then I noticed my mom walking toward us. She had a worried look on her face, too.

"Is something wrong?" she asked.

I didn't bother to answer—she knows how I feel about our trip tomorrow.

It was Ms. Perzana who piped up and said, "I was just wondering why Adam wasn't outside with his friends."

My mom bit her lip nervously. We've had some major scenes about going to the moon. I know that she didn't

want to get in a fight in front of half the neighborhood. She glanced over her shoulder toward the French doors, where my friends were gathered outside on the deck. She had on a bright red dress and her hair was done up nicely. Usually, I tell her when she looks especially good. But tonight, I hadn't said a word.

"Don't you want to join your friends, Adam?" she asked.

"Nope," I said, shaking my head firmly.

"Why not?"

What could I tell her? None of my friends understood how I felt. They all say they're going to miss me and stuff. But they think I should be excited about going to the moon. "Adam," they told me, "you're like one of those colonists who sailed across the ocean to settle new land." Yeah, well, that new land had trees and water and animals and . . . heck, that new land had air! There's not any air on the moon. Every time I want to take a stroll outside, I'm going to have to slip into a space suit and strap on a helmet. That should put a damper on the old social life.

"Look, there's Amie," my mom said as she pointed toward the fireplace. Amie was my favorite cousin. "She said she's been looking for you all . . ."

"I'm tired," I interrupted curtly. "I think I'll hit the sack."

With that, I rose and stalked out of the room. I didn't bother to say good-bye to anyone. Why should I? I wouldn't be seeing them for four long years. They probably wouldn't even remember me by the time we got back.

My mom came into the hall and stood at the bottom of the stairs, watching as I made my way up to my bedroom. Right before I walked inside my room, she called out, "Sweet dreams, Adam."

"Fat chance," I muttered under my breath.

I locked the door behind me and then fell onto the bed, face down in a pillow. I didn't want to see the room. It was bare. There wasn't anything left but my bed and a nightstand with a lamp. All my belongings had been packed away. Some would go with me to the moon, like my favorite clothes and music holodiscs. But most would stay in storage while we were gone. The house was already rented out to a family with kids. They had a teenage boy about the same age as me. He would be using this room for the next four years. I didn't like that. I had been raised in this house. And my bedroom had always been my place—my one place in the world where I could kick off my shoes and be myself. I can't remember how many nights my friends and I had stayed up in my room talking about cars and music and girls. Once you hit 12, it always comes down to girls, doesn't it? Regardless, I didn't like the thought of someone else sleeping here. But then, there wasn't anything I liked about going to the moon.

Maybe it would be different if we were taking the shuttle and spending a week there—or even a month. But we were going to live there for four years. Four long years. My entire high-school career would be spent on a rock. By the time we got back, I'd be heading off for college. By the time we got back, I doubted I'd ever want to speak to my parents again.

I punched the pillow and rolled over, feeling guilty about feeling mad at my parents. Deep down, I knew I was being unfair. I really couldn't blame my mom and dad for wanting to go. They had worked hard for this chance. In their minds, we were going to make history. I had tried hard to look at it that way. But I'm not a scientist. There'll be nothing for me to do up there. I can't race my airbike. I can't swim. I can't run track. I'll probably spend a gazillion hours playing computer games. And you know what's funny about that? My parents hate computer games. They say they turn your mind to mush.

I tossed and turned on the mattress. I could hear the party down below. But the noise wasn't really keeping me up—it was the thought of all those happy people, having a good time while I was so miserable. I was certain I'd be up all night. But eventually, I must have fallen off to sleep. The last thing I remember thinking was this:

Today is my last day on Earth.

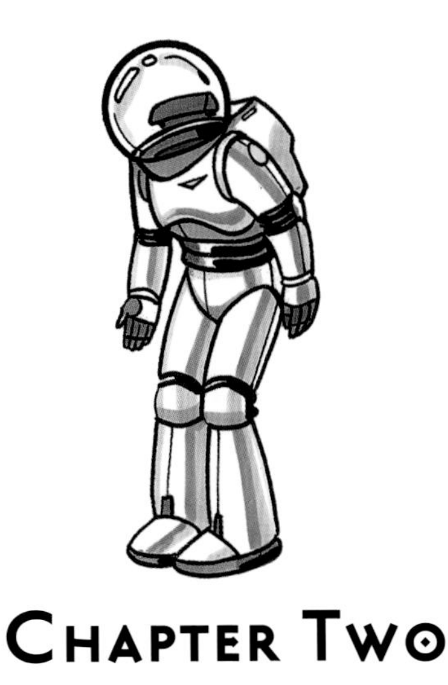

Chapter Two

At 5 A.M. on a Monday morning, most folks are still in bed. But the streets of our town were lined with people waving as we made our way to GOSC headquarters. We live near the space launch station, so it was a short drive. I sat in the back of our solar rider, taking in every face, every palm tree, every blade of grass. It's strange how you look at things differently when you know you won't be seeing them for a while. Even the fluorescent lines on the skyway fascinated me. There wouldn't be any skyways on the moon. Not unless we built them. I tried to picture myself in a bulky space suit, swinging a sledgehammer. Try as I might, I just couldn't see it.

"You hanging in there, babe?" my mom asked, turning around in her seat.

"Yeah, I'm fine," I said absently. I had caught a glimpse of the ocean. I was trying to freeze it in my mind so that I would never forget how it looked.

"You excited?" my dad asked, catching my eye in the rearview mirror.

I just looked at him. His face kind of fell and he turned his attention back to the skyway. My mom gave a soft sigh. Like my dad, she looked sad. And I realized then what I'd known all along—they loved me so much they couldn't really enjoy this experience unless I did, too. That made me feel ashamed.

"Will there be a lot of people at the launch?" I asked.

My parents perked up, just glad to hear me speak. I'd said so little to them in the last three months—since the day we had begun training for the moon—that we had almost lived like strangers.

"This is a pretty big deal—a first in space history. So I imagine there'll be quite a crowd," my dad answered. He paused, and then said, "You remember what I told you about the reporters?"

I nodded. "Before we suit up, we have to go to a press conference and they'll ask us lots of questions."

"That's right," my mom said. "But all you have to do is wave and smile. Nobody expects you to give a speech."

"I think I should give a speech," I teased. "I'll tell them how I just can't wait to get to the moon. I've spent the entire summer jumping up and down with joy."

We all laughed at that. It felt good to share a joke with my parents. We used to joke all the time. In fact, before this business with the moon came up, I used to hang out with them fairly often. I mean, I had friends and everything, but my mom and dad were the cool parents. So when the guys and I got together, we usually met at my house. Half the time, I'd find my buddies in the kitchen chatting with my folks. That's one reason why my friends couldn't understand how I felt—they'd give an arm and a leg to fly off into space with parents like mine.

"We're almost there," my dad said, pointing to a group of white buildings ahead.

I strained for a better view. The parking lot was jammed with vehicles. People were pulling picnic baskets and blankets from the trunks of their solar riders. A cop stood in the middle of the skyway, directing traffic. We were waved right through. My dad steered our rider into an underground parking lot. Three GOSC officials were there to open our doors. I recognized one—Admiral Longview, in charge of the moon project and my parents' boss. He had been at our house before. And I had heard my parents talk about him in whispers. He looked like a friendly, gray-haired uncle, but he was, apparently, one tough old guy.

"How is everyone feeling this morning?" he asked in a booming voice.

"Fine, sir," my dad said as he folded his long legs out of the vehicle.

"And you, Sherra?" The admiral turned to my mom.

"A few butterflies," she said, patting her stomach. "Otherwise, OK."

"You're a seasoned veteran," the admiral said reassuringly. "This is what? Your fifth trip in space?"

Mom nodded. "Yes, but I've never taken my son along before."

Laughing, the admiral ruffled my hair. "That's true," he conceded. "But this young man has the makings of a fine astronaut. I can see it in his eyes."

I blinked like you do when there's something in your eye that you're trying to get rid of. "How are you, son?" he continued. "Looking forward to your adventure?"

My parents looked on anxiously, half-expecting me to blurt out something awful. But I did them proud. I just smiled and said, "Yes, sir."

"Nervous, are you?"

Strangely enough, no one had ever asked me that before. I thought it over, and then gave him an honest answer.

"A little, I guess."

He nodded as though I had said something very wise. Putting an arm across my shoulders, he started to lead me toward the stairs. "It's normal to be nervous," he said as we walked. "In fact, I'd be worried if you weren't. You're exploring new territory, breaking new ground—going where no boy has ever gone before. Yes, it'll be exciting. But you mustn't think it's going to be all fun and games."

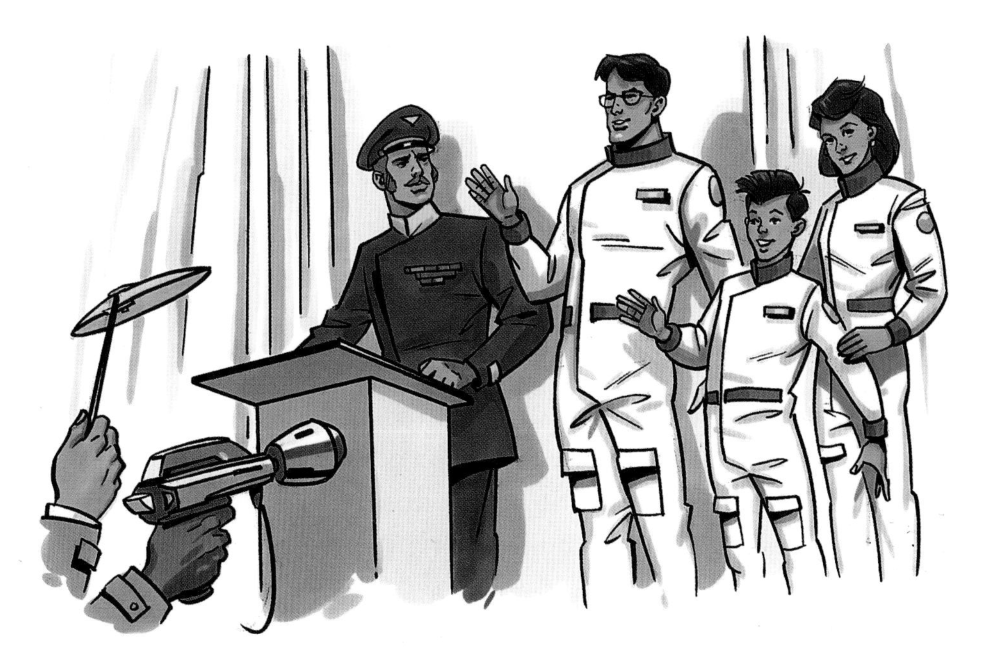

"I've never thought that," I assured him. Behind me, I heard my dad chuckle.

"So . . ." The admiral paused before a door at the top of the stairs. "Ready to face the press?"

My dad put a hand on my shoulder and slipped his other arm around my mom. "Ready, sir," he said.

The admiral opened the door. Directly in front of us was a platform with a podium.

Sitting in seats below the platform were about a hundred reporters armed with microphones, cameras, and recorders. They leapt to their feet when we entered. They started to shout out questions, but the admiral raised his hands, and they all quieted down like kids in a classroom.

"Before we open the floor to questions," the admiral said, "I'd like to say a few words. We don't have much time, so I'll keep it short. As you all know, our world is sadly struggling through a massive drought. Peace still reigns, but tensions are high due to the lack of resources available. In these troubled times, five nations have come together in a scientific venture of historic magnitude.

"The global divisions of Northland, Southland, Eastland, Westland, and Aqualand were each given the opportunity to select a delegate family to participate in the lunar habitat program. The countries of Umbria, Hadouth, Danja, Loover, and Grazia are sending their finest people—the best of the best—to build the first colony on the moon. I don't have to tell you what this means for the future of space travel—or, for that matter, for the very survival of the human race. We now have the power to populate other planets. More than that, we now have the power to forge a new spirit of cooperation and peace among nations. What you see in front of you," he said, pausing to wave a hand in our direction, "is a typical Umbrian family. But make no mistake about it—these people are heroes. Future generations will speak their names in awe. Ladies and gentlemen, let us be the first to honor them. I give you Dr. Samuel Carter, Dr. Sherra Carter, and Mr. Adam Carter."

Applause roared in my ears. My mom had warned me

that the reporters might ask some uncomfortable questions. But these people seemed more likely to throw flowers at our feet. I'll admit I was a little overwhelmed by it all. Luckily, I didn't have to say much. The only questions that came my way were things like:

"How ya feeling, Adam?"

"Fine, thanks."

"Looking forward to your first trip in space, Adam?"

"You bet."

"What do you think you'll like best about the moon, Adam?"

"Uh . . . let me think. The sunny beaches, I guess."

They laughed like I was some kind of famous comedian. Admiral Longview was beaming at me like I was his firstborn son. When they lined us up to take pictures, he planted himself in the middle and put me right in front of him. About a million flashbulbs went off. Still blinded by the lights, we were herded out the door.

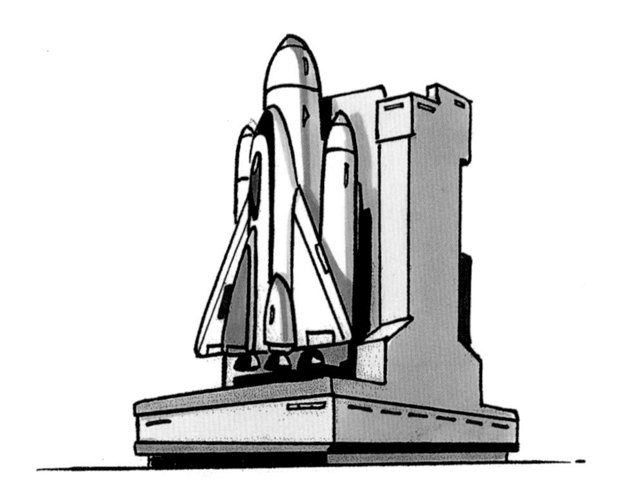

Chapter Three

Everything was a bit of a blur after that. Admiral Longview suddenly changed back into what he was: a tough, old soldier. He rushed us down a long, white hall, snapping orders at the half dozen GOSC employees who scrambled to keep up with us. We were still his precious cargo, but everyone else just seemed to be in his way.

"Is headquarters set to go?" he asked out of the right side of his mouth.

The woman near his right elbow glanced up from the notebook she was carrying. She and all the other GOSC people were wearing white coats—I felt like I was in a hospital. "Affirmative, sir," she answered.

"So we're on schedule?" the admiral asked out of the left side of his mouth.

The man near his left elbow said, "Yes, sir. Sixty minutes from liftoff."

The admiral stopped in front of a steel door and glanced at his watch. "You have exactly 30 minutes to suit up. Afterwards, you'll be led directly to the spacecraft." He paused to give my parents and me a searching look. Apparently satisfied that we weren't having second thoughts, he nodded once, then said, "This is where I leave you. From this point on, our only contact will be by radio. My best wishes go with you. Good luck to you all."

He shook my parents' hands, and then mine. Then he turned on his heel and marched away. It was an abrupt good-bye. But I had seen his eyes—they had been full of emotion. This project was his baby so I suppose we were kind of like family to him. I imagine he left fast to hide his soft side.

My dad opened the steel door and led us inside the room. Four GOSC technicians followed to help us suit up. Our space suits were hanging side by side on the wall. I had a sudden image of our bathrobes at home, lined up from largest to smallest, and I was hit by a wave of homesickness. My stomach twisted. For a second, I felt like throwing up. But then someone tugged on the sleeve of my jacket.

Things started moving fast again—too fast for me to feel sad.

All summer long, I had trained with my parents at GOSC. We had done the usual anti-gravity maneuvers and motion-sickness tests. We had even done simulated space walks and liftoffs. I had spent more time this summer in a space suit than in a bathing suit. So I knew the "suiting up" routine inside out. I didn't have to think—I just moved on automatic pilot—and it helped to calm my nerves.

I was the last one to slip on my helmet. Our GOSC helpers had to secure it to my space suit because I had on thick gloves. The second they stepped back, I heard my father's voice through the little speaker built inside the helmet near my ear.

"Can you hear me?" he asked.

I nodded. "Loud and clear," I said into my microphone.

"How's that suit feel?"

I lifted one leg up and shook it, and then I flexed my arms. The space suit looked bulky, but it was actually fairly lightweight. Even my boots were climate-controlled so I wasn't too hot or too cold. "I feel like I'm wrapped in a cloud," I told him.

He grinned, and then glanced at my mom. "And you?" he asked.

She gave him a thumbs up. "I'm doing fantastic," she said.

"Well then," my father said as he brought his gloved hands together, "let's get this show on the road."

It was a short march down a sloped hall to the door that led outside to the space pad. One of the GOSC people opened the door, then saluted briskly as my parents and I walked through. We paused on a metal platform and then suddenly, I heard a roar like ocean waves, muffled through my helmet. My mouth dropped open when I saw the crowd below us. There were thousands of people lined up against the metal fence that separated the public viewing area from the space pad. A lot of them carried hand-painted signs that said things like:

"GOOD LUCK, SAM, SHERRA, AND ADAM" or "UMBRIA IS PROUD OF OUR FIRST FAMILY IN SPACE."

All the people were cheering and waving. Like my parents, I waved back. I'll be honest—it was fun standing high up there on a platform with a bunch of people shouting out my name.

I had known there was a lot of excitement about this space trip. But my parents had wanted to keep things as normal as possible for me. So I hadn't spoken to reporters or anything like that. This was my first glimpse of all the hoopla. I wasn't sure if it made me want to fly to the moon. But it did make me realize that people weren't going to forget us up there.

"Ready to proceed?" one of the GOSC guys asked.

Just then, I caught sight of a group of my friends,

standing near the front of the fence. I had asked them not to show up; I didn't want any long good-byes. But they had come anyway. I felt half sad, half glad. Their sign read:

"DON'T FORGET TO WRITE, ADAM!"

My mom's gaze followed mine. She saw my friends and smiled. "I bet they'll be standing there, just like that, when we come home," she said.

I swallowed back the lump in my throat. "I hope so," I said, and even to my own ears, I sounded about five years old.

She took my hand. "Ready?" she asked gently.

I nodded. My mom slipped her arm through my dad's, and together we walked down the broad stairs that led to the space pad. Only then did I glance up at the spacecraft. It loomed over us like a huge, white mountain. The closer we got, the louder the crowd roared. But I barely heard them now. I was starting to feel nervous again. I mean, I trusted space flight—my parents had been going into space since I was little. But I knew that once I entered that thing, I would be leaving behind everything that mattered to me. I wanted to turn and run—in fact, I probably would have if all those eyes weren't watching me.

As it was, I just put one foot in front of the other. We crossed the concrete space pad and went up the metal steps to the gaping door of the spacecraft. I would have walked right inside if my dad hadn't stopped me. He turned me around for another wave at the cheering crowd. I didn't enjoy it this time. I just wanted to get the whole thing over with.

My dad tapped my shoulder and we entered.

From the outside, a spacecraft looks as big as a skyscraper. But the booster rockets and fuel tanks make up most of the craft. The part that the astronauts stay in is fairly small. In our craft, there was a room with a control panel and four seats. Behind that was another room with four bunks. We didn't need more space than that. It would only take five hours to get to the moon, and all our belongings had been transported ahead of us.

To my surprise, there was already a woman suited up in the control room. Then I remembered—it was Major Hinley, our pilot.

"You should have joined us outside," my father said as he took the seat next to her.

"Oh, this is your show," she said, smiling. "I didn't want to steal your thunder."

She and my mom were old friends, and they talked quietly about other flights they had taken together. I could hear them through my headset, but I didn't listen to the words. I was trying to make my mind blank while a GOSC technician strapped me into my seat. It was too late to argue about leaving, and there was no use worrying about what might lie ahead. Better not to think at all, I told myself.

"You OK?" Major Hinley asked when the technician was through.

I nodded.

"Ten minutes until liftoff," she said.

I really don't know what went through my mind during those last few minutes on Earth. It was like I was outside myself, watching a movie with me in a starring role. I remember that the GOSC people wished us luck and then left the spacecraft. I heard a grating sound as the outside door was latched and the rocket supports were rolled away. Through my headset, ground control was guiding the pilot. They spoke in short, calm sentences. I watched as the pilot pushed a switch here, flicked a button there. Then I heard a deep voice say:

"Ten, nine, eight . . ."

There was a loud whoosh as the rockets fired up. The spacecraft began to shudder.

". . . six, five, four . . ."

I squeezed my eyes shut and gripped the arms of my chair.

". . . two, one, liftoff!"

Chapter Four

Did you ever wonder what it's like to be an insect hanging onto the windshield of a vehicle that's speeding down a skyway? Well, that's what it's like to lift off in a spacecraft. You're pressed back against the seat—it feels like the skin on your cheeks is stretched behind your ears. Everything's rattling, even your teeth. And the rockets aren't just loud—they're deafening. We didn't try to talk. We just hung on to our seats. Right when I was sure my bones would fall apart and my eyes would pop out, I felt a jolt as the booster rockets slipped away. All of a sudden, we were gliding as smooth as eagles.

We were in outer space.

"That wasn't so bad, was it?" Major Hinley asked as she stripped off her gloves and tugged at her helmet.

"Not at all," my mom said, pulling off her own helmet.

By this time, my dad was already helmet-free and was working on mine. I took a deep gulp of air when my helmet came off. I could feel the sweat rolling down my cheeks and my eyes were as wide as UFOs.

"Adam?" my dad said worriedly. "Adam, speak to me."

I blinked once, twice. Then I grinned. "What a trip!" I yelled.

They all laughed. "You liked that, did you?" Major Hinley asked.

I nodded vigorously. "It was like a rollersky ride, only better."

Just then the radio on the control board came to life. "This is headquarters. Come in, MoonLab."

MoonLab was the name of our spacecraft. Major Hinley hit a switch, then sat back. "We read you, headquarters. Come back."

"Report your status, MoonLab."

"We've reached an altitude of 700 kilometers and climbing. All systems go."

There was the sound of clapping over the radio—the control room was celebrating another successful launch. Then a voice said, "Roger that, MoonLab. How's our little greenhorn?"

I scowled. I knew what a greenhorn was—it's what they used to call people a long time ago who went to unexplored lands without knowing a thing about surviving in the wild.

Major Hinley gave me a wink. "At last count," she said to the radio, "our greenhorn has been in space more times than you. You want to drop that nickname?"

There was a chuckle over the radio. "Roger that, MoonLab. Give the greenhorn . . . uh, give young Adam my apologies. And tell him that he just made the cover of X-Teen magazine."

"X-Teen?" I gasped. The last person on that cover was the world's coolest rock guitarist.

Major Hinley hit another switch and a screen on the control board lit up. We were instantly linked to headquarters by camera. I saw a guy sitting at the control board, holding up a magazine with my face on the cover.

I squinted my eyes and turned my head this way and that, checking it out. Then I grinned.

I gotta admit, I looked good.

"Hit the stands an hour ago—already sold out," the guy said as he lowered the magazine.

"There aren't any left?" I asked, disappointed.

"I can send this one with the next cargo mission."

"That'll be great."

"Anything else you want?"

I thought for a moment. "How about some Cocobars?"

The guy covered his mouth with his hand, but his smile still showed. "Roger that, MoonLab. One box of Cocobars set for the next flight up."

With that, headquarters signed off and I sat back, thinking. Since I had first found out about this trip, I had been dead set against it. I hadn't shown any interest, let alone asked any questions. Now, I found myself wondering: what's it going to be like?

"Mom?"

She glanced up from her laptop computer—she's the colony's head engineer and she spends all her free moments working and reworking building plans. "Yeah, Adam?" she said.

"When we get there . . ."

She tilted her head, waiting.

". . . well, what will we see?"

She shut off her computer and turned to face me. "Well, the first thing we'll see is a big, long stretch of dusty ground—we have to land pretty far from the colony because we don't want to damage the structure."

"So there's something up there already?"

She nodded. "The outer shell of the colony is complete—technical crews have been working on it for nearly two years. From the outside, it looks like a big sports arena—you know, one of those domes where they play astroball? Inside, though, there's still a lot to be done. Our sleeping quarters are ready and there's a kitchen and a bathroom. But it's more like a dorm environment—at first, all the families will be in one big room. Part of my job is to make it feel like a neighborhood enclosed under one large shell."

"Wait a minute." I raised my hand. "Back up a second. Did you say that all the families are going to live in one big room?"

She smiled. "I know. I'm not crazy about it, either. For the first month or so, I imagine we'll be getting on each other's nerves. But the harder we work as a group, the sooner we'll have our own living spaces."

"I don't know anything about building," I pointed out.

"Oh, Adam, no one expects you to work. If you want to pitch in, that's fine. But we have enough adults to finish the job. Your main job will be going to school. We have a tutor for you and the other children. And we'll build a classroom so that it feels just like home."

I thought this over. It seemed kind of pointless to go all the way to the moon just to do what I did at home. "What if I want to help build?" I asked.

My mom looked pleased. "Every hand will be welcome," she said. Then her face turned stern. "But studying always . . ."

". . . comes first," I finished. She had said that line so many times before that I knew it by heart. "Are any of the other families there yet?"

She shook her head. "Umbria contributed the most money and resources to this project. So it was jointly agreed that our family would arrive first. The Southland delegation will leave tomorrow. By the end of the week, all five families will be on the moon."

"How many kids?" I asked.

"A total of nine."

"Any boys my age?"

She hesitated, then said, "There's a girl who's about . . ."

"Mom," I interrupted firmly, "you're not answering my question."

Sighing, she said, "The boy closest to your age is 10."

Ten? I sat back, frowning. A ten-year-old wasn't going to be any fun. What could I do with him? Baby-sit?

My dad put his hand on my arm. He'd been quietly following the conversation. He did that a lot with my mom and me. And he usually only jumped in when he felt I was about to give her a hard time. "You know," he started to say, "the Hadouth girl is your age . . ."

"She probably doesn't speak Umbrian," I muttered.

My dad drew back. "Actually, she does," he said. "And I'm sure that at this moment, she's complaining to her parents that you don't speak her language. Seems to me, son, that if anyone has a right to be disappointed, she does."

If he was trying to make me feel bad, he succeeded. I already felt guilty for complaining about the Southland girl and I hadn't even met her yet. I knew that when I did finally face her, I would go out of my way to be nice. That's what guilt did to me.

My dad knew me well. His face softened as he read my thoughts and he reached out to ruffle my hair.

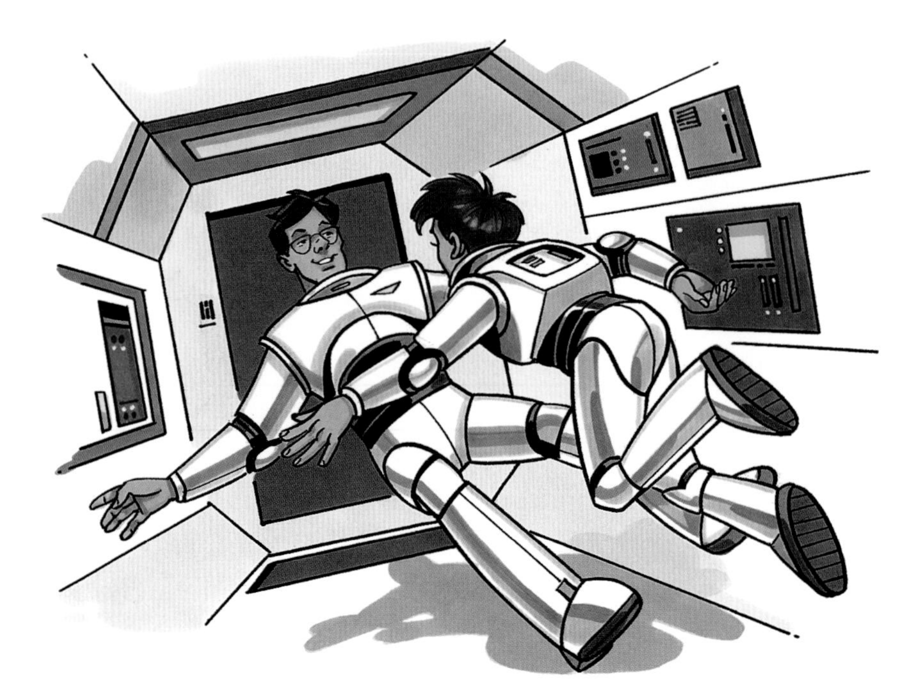

"How about a float?" he asked.

I looked at him, confused. A float was something that old-timers used to drink. "What are you talking about?"

Eyes twinkling, he said, "Watch this." He unbuckled the straps on his seat and then pushed himself up. And just like that, he was floating through the room.

With the liftoff and everything, I had forgotten about gravity—that is, I'd forgotten that I'd left gravity behind. My hands scrambled to unbuckle my straps. The second I was free, I was floating after my dad.

We did somersaults. We did cartwheels. We did handstands on the ceiling. Major Hinley had a camera that was linked by satellite to Earth. She started to film us, and all across Umbria—all across the world—people laughed along with us. Who knew outer space could be so fun? I was having the time of my life until Major Hinley lowered the camera and said:

"Time to buckle up."

We had 30 minutes, she had added solemnly, until moon landing.

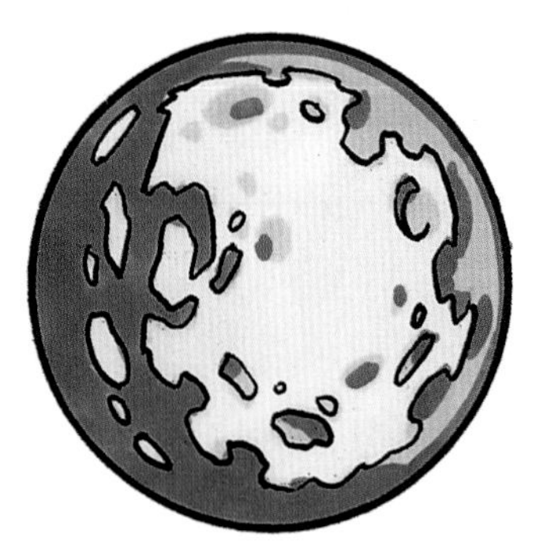

Chapter Five

Landing on the moon was nowhere near as fun as taking off from Earth. The only part I liked was watching the moon get closer and closer. At first, it was nothing but a round ball in the sky—just the same old moon that you see every night. But then it seemed to grow until it filled the whole window of the spacecraft. I could see every mark on its jagged surface. I couldn't tear my eyes away. I didn't even realize that I was leaning forward in my seat until Major Hinley put her hand on my arm.

"Sit back," she said. "It's time to maneuver."

Maneuver? What did that mean? Before I could ask, Major Hinley pointed the nose of the spacecraft straight up. Now we were facing an inky sky full of stars. The moon was behind us. Slowly, we eased down backwards to its surface.

Bump.

We had landed.

I thought, that's it? And then it hit me—I'm on the moon! I am the first kid in the history of the universe to be here!

Just like that, I forgot that I hadn't wanted to go on this trip. I forgot everything, including the procedures that we had learned back on Earth. I knew that I couldn't just leap out onto the moon. Still, I was halfway out of my seat before Major Hinley stopped me.

"We have to report to headquarters, then wait for the lunar rover to arrive," she explained.

Sighing, I sat back. We were still facing up toward the sky; I couldn't see the moon at all. I tried to look sideways, but my headrest blocked the view. My knee started to bounce like it always does when I'm feeling impatient. My mom patted my arm reassuringly.

"It'll only be a few minutes," she promised.

I nodded and did my best not to squirm. Major Hinley was confirming the landing with headquarters. I swear it took an hour, but it was probably more like five minutes. At one point, my dad tapped my shoulder and I realized that the control room crew was congratulating me.

"Thank you," I said politely while my knee bounced up and down. Looking back, I think that was the most exciting part of the trip—those long minutes spent waiting in the spacecraft. I'm the kind of guy who likes to jump right into things. But you can't do that on the moon. There are all sorts of safety steps you have to follow. And even if you could bypass those steps, you still couldn't rush around. So everything's in slow motion. When the lunar rover finally arrived, we had to move like snails toward the door. We held on to the craft's metal framework so that we wouldn't float in the wrong direction. As we waited for the major to unlatch the door, my dad saw the pained look on my face and he laughed.

"Patience, my son, patience," he said.

Well, I was trying to be patient. But the door had one of those complicated wheel locks and it took forever to open it. I was standing right in the threshold when the metal door finally slid aside.

My jaw dropped to the floor.

I'd seen pictures of the moon, just like every other kid in school. But pictures don't compare to the real thing. I mean, I knew the moon's surface was brown. But when you look around and all you see is brown, brown, everywhere, it hits you, it really hits you—you're not on Earth anymore.

There aren't any houses or trees. No grass, no billboards. There wasn't a sign of human beings anywhere, not even a tiny footprint in the dust.

There were rocks, though—plenty of rocks. Some formed small piles. Some stood alone like mighty guards. Others rose into sheer mountains. And in between all the rocks were smooth, shallow craters that looked like giant, dried-up mud puddles.

We had landed in one of those craters. Major Hinley pushed a button and a metal ramp suddenly appeared, stretching from the spacecraft to the ground. My dad tapped my shoulder and pointed to the ramp.

"Me first?" I asked.

He nodded. "You bet."

I took one cautious step forward. Then I thought, what the heck, and jumped from the ramp to the ground. Like I said before, everything happens on the moon in slow motion. I could have recited the alphabet by the time I landed on the ground.

My mom laughed. "And you thought the moon wasn't going to be any fun," she teased.

As my parents and Major Hinley made their way down the ramp, I caught a movement out of the corner of my eye. I turned to look. Beyond the rim of the crater, I could see something approaching. At first, it looked like a big white bug crawling over the rocks. And even though I knew that there weren't any alien life forms on the moon, my heart skipped a beat. Then I realized it was the lunar rover, coming to take us to the colony.

Major Hinley had her camera in her hands. All our actions, including my jump off the ramp, were being televised live on Earth. Now she turned the lens on the driver. He pulled alongside of us, leaving deep, wide tracks in the dusty surface. When he saw the camera, he chuckled at the major.

"Hey director, do you know where I can find the pilot of this spacecraft?" he asked.

"Movie-making happens to be my favorite hobby," she countered smoothly. "So I volunteered to document the project. Now be a good boy and smile nice for the camera."

He wasn't just smiling—he was beaming. He turned to my parents and me and said, "I'm Captain Juarez, your chauffeur for the evening. Where would you folks like to go? The Hilton? The Hyatt? The Ritz?"

"What a ham," Major Hinley muttered to no one in particular. To Captain Juarez, she added, "Keep up the bad jokes and I'm cutting you out of my film."

The captain shrugged good-naturedly. Then he held out his hand to my dad. "Welcome to the moon, sir."

We shook hands all around, and then we piled into the rover. I sat in back with my parents. The rover climbed over the rim of the crater like it was a little bump in the road.

It scrambled over rocks and down steep canyons. It was the most powerful off-road vehicle I'd ever been in. I was thinking how badly I'd like to get behind the wheel, when my dad said, "Look over there."

I turned to see a huge blue orb rising over the horizon. It was covered with a wispy layer of white. It took me a second to realize—that's Earth. Surprisingly enough, I didn't feel sad. I just felt this huge wave of pride. I can honestly say I'd never seen anything so beautiful as my home planet. All the rest of the planets—even Saturn with its rings—well, you can't imagine anything living on them. But then you look at good old, blue Earth and you know, *you know,* that there are hearts beating there.

"Now look straight ahead," my dad said.

I turned. "What . . ." I started. Then my eyes grew round. "Wow," I whispered.

Right in front of us, rising high above the rocky surface, was the Moon Colony. Mom was right—it was shaped like a dome. But it was the biggest dome I'd even seen. It covered about four hectares.

It was made of a thin, transparent material that looked very fragile, like you could tear it apart with your hands. But I knew the material was strong. GOSC had tested it back on Earth—a meteoroid could land on that dome and it would bounce right off.

"Home sweet home," Captain Juarez said as he pulled up next to the colony.

My mom got out first. “Isn’t it amazing?” she said in an awed voice.

“It sure is,” my dad said, joining her. He put an arm around her waist and they both stood staring up at the dome. They had been working on this project for years. I knew they needed a moment to absorb the fact that it wasn’t a dream anymore. It was an honest-to-gosh reality. As for me, I was just anxious to see the inside. So I walked ahead with Captain Juarez. Five GOSC technicians were waiting for us by the door.

“You must be Adam,” the tallest one said as he shook my hand.

I nodded. It occurred to me that I’d shaken more hands today than I had in my entire life.

“I’m Captain Johnson,” the man continued. “I’m the crew leader of the construction team. Your mom will be my boss.”

“Pleased to meet you,” I said in a distracted voice. I was trying to look around his side to see into the dome.

“And this is . . .”

He introduced the rest of the team. I forgot their names as soon as he said them. I know that sounds rude. But the truth is, adults can stretch things on forever while kids just want to cut to the quick. I wanted to see where I was going to live for the next four years. I didn’t want to shake any more hands.

The only one who seemed to understand how I felt was Captain Juarez. While the team was being introduced to my parents, he came up behind me and said:

"First one inside gets to choose his bunk."

I raced toward the door. Through my headset, I heard Major Hinley shout, "Adam. Wait! I want to get this on film . . ."

But I was already through the door.

Chapter Six

I don't mean to sound like a constant complainer. But I thought the inside of the dome would be huge. I mean, that's what it looked like from the outside. But long sheets of plastic blocked off most of the inner dome. The only open area was about the size of a gym. There was a containment room right by the door—that's where you took off your space suit. To the right, there was a kitchen with your basic equipment—stove, refrigerator, and cupboards. The table was huge, with about 25 chairs. Next to the table was the bathroom. It was nothing more than a toilet, sink, and shower surrounded by four pieces of plywood that passed for walls.

The rest of the inside—the part that wasn't blocked off by plastic—was the sleeping quarters. The crew had built plywood partitions to separate the sleeping quarters into about two dozen small rooms. Each room had a dresser and a cot. One blanket, one pillow—that was it.

It was like camp, only worse.

I had already "unsuited," but I still had my helmet in my hand. I let it fall to the floor. I was vaguely aware of my parents behind me. As they unsuited, my mom was going on about the crew's "excellent work."

"You've gotten so much done!" she gushed. "I didn't expect all this progress."

Progress?

I turned to face her. She could tell by my expression that I was not a happy camper. Even Major Hinley seemed to realize that this wasn't a moment to share with the masses—she quickly lowered her camera.

"We came to the moon for this?" I demanded, waving a hand around.

"Adam . . ." my mom started.

But I cut her off. "I don't care what you say—it's awful. And I'm not staying here for four years."

Before anyone could react, I turned and stomped away. I went to the farthest room and plopped down on a cot. My heart was pounding. I had just yelled at my mother. We disagreed sometimes. We even argued now and then. But I rarely, if ever, yelled at her.

I heard footsteps coming toward my cubicle. They weren't light like my mom's footsteps. They were solid like my dad's. I winced. Given a choice, I'd rather face an angry mom than an angry dad.

And boy, was he angry. He stalked into my cubicle. The room was small and he's a big guy—it seemed like he filled the whole space.

He stood over me with his hands planted on his hips. "Adam," he said, "for the past three months, your mother and I have been nothing but patient. We listened, day in and day out, while you whined and complained. And do you know why?"

I shook my head meekly. From experience, I knew it was best not to speak at times like this. "Because we respect you," he continued sternly. "Your opinions matter to us. As your parents, we both agree that you have the right to express yourself. That does not, however, give you the right to yell at your mother. You will never use that tone of voice with her again. Is that understood, young man?"

I gulped. "Yes, sir."

"Now you will march out there and apologize to your mother. And you will also apologize to the men and women whose hard work you so rudely insulted."

I stood and began walking out of the room. As I passed him, he said, "One more thing."

I turned. "Yes, sir?"

"If you make up your mind that this whole experience will be a disaster, then trust me, it will. Adam . . ." He paused and his face softened slightly. "Adam, I know this is hard on you. But you have the power to make it better. Not me, not your mother, only you."

"How?" I asked, truly puzzled.

He sighed and I knew I had disappointed him again. I thought he might walk away. Instead, he said, "OK, we'll start simple. You've spent a lot of time focusing on what you don't like about this project, right?"

I nodded. No argument there.

"Tonight before you go to sleep, I want you to spend a few minutes—just a few minutes out of the day—focusing on what you *like* about being here. Make a list. Write it down. And when you get up in the morning, the first thing I want you to do is read that list. Agreed?"

"OK," I said.

To be honest, I didn't see how it would help. But that's not something you tell a dad who just got over being mad.

I mentioned before that I'm the kind of guy who likes to move fast. There's one exception to this rule: in the morning when I wake up, I don't want to move at all. My alarm clock usually goes off about five times before I get up. Then I want to take about an hour to stretch and another hour to shower and dress.

During the school year, this drives my mom crazy—she has to pound on my door to get me up. But during the summer, she lets it slide and I might linger in bed until noon. Technically, it was still summer—back home, I wouldn't be starting school for another two weeks. But maybe my dad was still sore from the night before. He was in my cubicle bright and early, shouting, "Get up!"

"Wha . . . Huh?" I rolled over, mumbling.

"I said, get out of bed. We've got a lot to do today."

I propped myself up on my elbows. Through bleary eyes, I gazed around the cubicle. Where the heck was I? Oh, yeah, I was on the moon. With an effort, I focused on my dad, who was standing in the doorway with an expectant look on his face.

"What time is it?" I asked him.

"Eight o'clock."

"Ah, geez." I collapsed back on the pillow.

"Adam, get up," he said firmly. "The Southland family will be here in one hour. I expect you to be dressed and waiting to greet them by the door."

"OK, OK." I threw back the blanket and sat up. My bathrobe was hanging on a hook near the doorway. I shuffled over and slipped it on. I started to walk past my dad, but he stopped me.

"Hold on a minute," he said. "Aren't you forgetting something?"

"Uh . . ." I patted the pockets in my bathrobe. I had no idea what I was looking for. I'll be honest—I'm not the brightest light in the morning.

"The list," my dad said with just the slightest touch of annoyance in his voice. "Did you make out the list last night like I asked you?"

"Oh, yeah." I pointed to the dresser where a small piece of paper lay among my things. "There it is."

"Read it before you take a shower," he directed. Then he walked away.

Sighing, I picked up the paper and sat down on the cot. My list of what I liked about being here:

1. SEEING THE MOON UP CLOSE
2. RIDING IN THE LUNAR ROVER
3. SEEING EARTH FROM FAR AWAY

It wasn't much of a list. But I had racked my brains last night and it was the best I could come up with. I could have added things just to please my dad—things like, "I love my room" or "I enjoy new experiences." But I was guessing that my dad wanted me to be honest. Whatever he thought this list would do for me probably wouldn't work if I lied. I put it back on the dresser and headed for the shower.

Breakfast was surprisingly good. We had a cheese omelet, whole-wheat toast, orange juice, and berries swimming in a bowl of cream. I guess I had expected freeze-dried food. But Captain Juarez, who doubled as the chef, explained that fresh food was being sent up from Earth on a weekly basis.

"Each week, a different country will supply the food," he explained as he took a seat next to me at the table. "So one week, we'll have Umbrian. The next week, we'll have Danjan. The next week . . . well, you get the picture."

"What do Hadouthians eat?" I asked.

He frowned as he took a sip of coffee. "I'm not sure," he admitted. "But I'm cooking it, so I can make it taste like anything I want. What do you like to eat?"

"Pizza."

"Well then, whatever they give me, it'll come out tasting like pizza," he said. We toasted—he with his mug of coffee and I with my glass of orange juice. Just then, Major Hinley walked into the dome. She was suited up and had her helmet tucked under her arm.

"OK, everybody look smart," she said curtly. "The Hadouthians are here."

Chapter Seven

Major Hinley wanted everything to be perfect for the cameras. She decided that she and Captain Juarez would escort the Southlanders from the landing site to the colony. The rest of the crew would meet them outside the dome. She wanted my parents and me to remain inside and greet the newcomers in the kitchen. I knew she meant well, but the whole thing felt sort of unreal—like we were all extras on a movie set. And everyone was supposed to smile on cue and act friendly.

At 9:00 A.M. sharp, the lunar rover pulled up outside. Through the thin material that made up the dome, I saw a figure jump out of the rover and immediately hold up a camera—that had to be Major Hinley. She filmed the three Southlanders as they stepped out of the vehicle. Then the crew came forward and there was handshaking all around. Meanwhile, I was shifting from foot to foot. I was anxious to meet the only other teenager on the moon. But as usual, the adults were taking forever.

Major Hinley finally led the way into the containment room. The Hadouthian family took off their space suits, then stepped into the kitchen. The first one I saw was the father. He was a chemist. His name was Oscar Placker. He was as tall as my dad, but a lot stockier. He looked more like a boxer than a scientist.

The mother, on the other hand, had one of those tiny gymnast figures. She was a biologist and her name was Mata. She was introducing her daughter to my mom. The girl's face was turned away from me. Then she turned to shake my dad's hand and I caught my breath.

Honestly, she was the prettiest girl I'd ever seen.

Her name, I learned, was Natasha. She had long beautiful hair, high cheekbones, and sparkling eyes. She was tall like her dad but slender like her mom. Anyway, she was really polite to my parents and I could tell they liked her. When she was introduced to me, she looked me square in the eye and I could feel myself blushing.

"Pleased to meet you, Adam," she said in perfect Umbrian. "I hope we'll be good friends."

I mumbled "hi" and kept my eyes on the ground. My dad looked at me, frowning. He was waiting for me to say something coherent. But my mind was blank. It didn't help that the camera was rolling. I could feel sweat trickling down my back. My dad nudged me and I gulped and said, "So . . . uh . . . you're from Southland?"

It was a dumb question and I blushed even harder as

soon as the words came out of my mouth. But Natasha just nodded politely and said, "We're from the city of Carra, actually. Do you know where that is?"

"Yeah . . . it's, uh . . . it's cold there, right?"

Gee, I was getting dumber by the second. I was sure Natasha thought I was an idiot. But then she gave a quick glance at the camera. And when she looked back at me, she rolled her eyes discreetly as if to say, isn't this whole thing ridiculous?

"Yes, Carra's very cold," she said in a serious voice while her eyes sparkled mischievously. "We have lots of snow. Do you like snow?"

"I love snow," I said, already more relaxed with her.

"Cross-country skiing's one of my favorite sports."

"Mine, too," she said and a sad look crossed her face.

Just then I realized—I wasn't the only one who was homesick. She probably didn't want to be here any more than I did. I know this sounds awful, but even though I knew she'd rather be with her friends, I was glad she was here. She'd likely be the only person who could understand how I felt.

I started to ask her about the flight up, but her father turned to Major Hinley and said, "Could we have a moment without the camera?"

"Of course." The major lowered the camera.

To my parents, Dr. Placker said, "Perhaps it would be a good time for young Adam to show Natasha around."

Natasha and I glanced at each other. We both knew what her father was saying—the adults had serious things to discuss and they didn't want us kids around. I showed Natasha the bathroom, and then she followed me toward the sleeping quarters. There really wasn't much to see. I pointed out my room and then I shrugged.

"There you have it—that's the grand tour," I said.

"Which room is mine?" she asked.

"Any one you want, I guess."

"I'll take that one," she said, pointing across the hall from mine. Then she turned to gaze up at the long sheets of plastic that blocked off most of the inner dome. "What's behind there?" she asked.

"Come on, I'll show you," I said.

Last night after dinner, Captain Juarez had taken me behind the plastic, just like I was doing with Natasha now. The crew would start work later this morning on individual apartments for the five families who would live in the colony. There was a lot of construction material lying on the concrete floor.

Stacks of boards were next to rolls of carpet, and sheets of drywall were propped against the walls. Each apartment would have two bedrooms, a kitchen, a bath, and a living room. They also planned to build a library, a schoolroom, and a common room—a place where we could all get together and watch movies and stuff. When the work was done, the crew was going to dismantle the current sleeping quarters and turn the space into a rec area where we kids could play sports.

"What do you think?" I asked her.

She wrinkled her nose. "Well . . ."

I laughed. "Yeah, I know. It's sort of a mess now. But I've seen the blueprints. It won't look half bad when it's done."

She nodded absently. "Adam, can I ask you something?"

"Sure."

"Do you like being here?"

I shook my head. "Not really. But I didn't have a choice, you know? I mean, I'm 14. My parents weren't going to let me stay home by myself."

"Same here," she said as she settled on a stack of wooden boards. "I didn't want to come. I even asked if I could stay with my grandmother. But my parents didn't want to be away from me for four years. And I suppose I can understand that—especially after what happened right before we left Earth."

I sat down next to her. "What happened?" I asked.

Her eyes grew wide. "You don't know?"

I shook my head.

"The global drought has taken a turn for the worse," she said. "It mainly affected the Eastland Division. Right now, all of the countries that are involved in the Moon Colony are fine. But people are saying that this could affect the whole world."

"Oh, no." I took a moment to absorb the news. I didn't know much about global climate or natural disasters. But I did know that a long time ago, many countries had suffered terrible droughts, and their economies had collapsed. Countries battled over resources such as water and crops. Many of the countries not affected by the droughts refused to come to the aid of those suffering, which resulted in tension and animosity. Creation of the global divisions helped ease these tensions as Earth slowly recuperated. A lot of people lost their jobs and went hungry. I thought of my friends back home and felt sick to my stomach.

"Is that what your dad wanted to speak to my parents about?" I asked.

Natasha nodded. "My parents were given top secret papers to pass on to your parents. I'm not sure what the papers say. But I do know that for the time being, the leaders of our countries have decided to present a united front. When the rest of the families arrive, they want all the colonists to give a press conference, stressing the need to remain calm."

I shook my head, confused. "But what good would that do?" I asked. "I mean, why would anyone listen to us?"

"Because people back on Earth are excited about this project. Everyone feels a part of it, even if his or her own country isn't involved. Don't you see? The Moon Colony has brought people together. And they're holding the press conference to remind people of the good things we can accomplish when we pull together. They want to . . ." She gestured with her hands. ". . . make sure that no one panics. That would only make things worse."

"I guess that makes sense," I said. Still I doubted a press conference could stop people from panicking. My mind was racing ahead—an awful thought occurred to me and I started to share it with Natasha. Then I heard my dad call my name. "We'd better join them," I said instead.

As we walked past the cubicles, I decided not to tell her the thought that had crossed my mind seconds before. I didn't want to scare her. I didn't want her to realize that if the drought caused the economies of our countries to collapse, there was a good chance that we could end up stranded on the moon forever.

Chapter Eight

Throughout the rest of the week, there was a sort of tense, expectant atmosphere on the moon. Each morning we would get up and greet another new family. During the day, we'd work together in the dome. At night after dinner, we'd gather around the satellite hook-up and watch the news from Earth. Then we'd all go to bed, worrying about our friends and family back home.

The situation was getting worse. At first, only Eastland Division countries were affected. By the time the last family arrived on Friday, 10 other countries from all of the divisions were on the brink of financial ruin. Our countries—the countries that were building the Moon Colony—were still fine. And that seemed to make the other countries mad. They thought that the rich countries should help bail out the ones that were in trouble. They even started to say things about the Moon Colony—like how it was a big waste of money and resources.

Up on the moon, everyone seemed to have a different opinion about what should be done. Last night as we watched the news, Dr. Wingee, the Danjan physicist, said that the best thing to do was to let the drought run its course. Shipping countless amounts of food into the faltering countries would only weaken the reserves of the other, healthier countries, he said. My dad objected.

"That's a simplistic view," he argued. "We have a global economy now. If we don't take steps to help the drought victims now—if we ignore the problem—it will only hit us harder in the long run."

Natasha's mother jumped in, saying that the GOSC should take a strong stance and defend the Moon Colony. But then the Grazian astronomer, Dr. Smithfield, said that would only make things worse. GOSC, she insisted, should lie low.

It went on and on and their voices grew louder and louder. I remember thinking that just two nights ago, these people had held a press conference where they had stressed the need to pull together and to remain calm. As I watched them, my stomach started twisting. I went to bed early.

Things were no better the next morning at breakfast. The adults were barely speaking to each other. They ate in silence, then filed off to work on the inner dome. We kids cleared the table, then went to our cubicles to gather up our schoolbooks. It was Monday, our first day

of school. Until the inner dome was finished, we were going to study at the kitchen table. Captain Juarez was our tutor. He stood at the head of the table, watching as we shuffled down the hall to slump back in our seats.

"You're a lively group," he said, gazing around the table.

He was being sarcastic, of course. All of us kids were in various stages of depression. The Grazian twins—Harry and Jerry—were scribbling half-heartedly in their notebooks. They were 9 years old and if one was sad, the other was, too. The Danjan boy, Saul, was 10. He had his elbows on the table and his head propped in his hands. He looked about as glum as a kid could be. His sister, Lee, was 7. Her eyes were lowered and her arms were tight around the rag doll that she carried everywhere.

The Loover girl, Suzca, was 12. She had her head held high and her shoulders squared. She was trying to be brave because her younger siblings—Kyle, who was 9, and Joss, who was 8—were looking to her for direction. If she acted scared, then they'd be scared, too.

As for Natasha and me, we looked bored out of our minds. But our attitude was just a front. Underneath it all, I think Natasha felt like I did—a little worried, a little disgusted, a little scared.

"Anybody want to talk about what's going on here?" the captain asked as he took a seat.

We looked around at each other, but nobody piped up.

"Well then, I'll do the talking," the captain said.

"I imagine everyone's a little worried about the situation back home. You're scared for the people you left behind. And you're probably more than a little disgusted with the way the adults are acting here."

We all straightened. He had gotten our attention. In fact, it was as though he had read our minds.

"Am I on the right track?" he asked.

"Yes," Natasha answered while the rest of us nodded.

"The question is, what are you going to do about it?"

Captain Juarez stood up and walked to the far corner

of the room. I think he wanted us to think for ourselves and come up with a plan.

"What can we do?" I countered, jumping up from my seat.

He raised his shoulders, then let them drop. "That's completely up to you," he said, walking around the room. "Do you like how your parents are acting?"

"Of course not," I said.

"Well then, tell them. You're members of this colony—you have just as much right to speak up as anyone else."

Suzca laughed. "I don't know about your parents," she said to Captain Juarez, "but mine don't really enjoy hearing me speak up."

"Now that depends on how you approach them," the captain insisted. "If you use a reasonable tone, I'm sure they would listen."

"Why don't you talk to them for us?" Saul asked.

"Because I'm their cook," he explained, touching his shirt as he spoke. "And I'm their children's tutor. I'm someone who basically works for them. They look at me as an employee. They look at you as someone whose love they treasure and whose respect they want."

We all thought about that as the captain stood and rubbed his hands together. "Enough serious business for the day," he said. "How about a little field trip?"

In record time, we were suited up and standing outside near the lunar rovers. None of us had been out of the dome since we had arrived. We were all pretty excited about the prospect of exploring the moon's surface.

All of us were excited, that is, except little Lee. "Are you sure we're allowed to do this?" she asked the captain for the fifth time.

He patted her helmet. "Trust me, Lee. Your parents said it was fine. You just stay glued to my side, OK?"

With that, he picked Lee up and put her in the front seat of the rover. Then he turned to me and said, "We need to take two rovers. Do you think you can handle one of these things?"

"Do I?" I leapt about five feet for joy. That was the fun thing about the moon—when you jump, you really jump. "Hand over the keys," I said eagerly.

Laughing, he said, "There aren't any keys. Just push this button here and . . ."

He walked me through the gears. It wasn't that different from my airbike at home. Natasha sat in front with me. Suzca and her siblings were in back. Saul, Lee, and the twins went with the captain. I followed his rover down a small valley, then up over a hill and into a crater. We did crazy-eight figures in the smooth dust of the crater. The rovers didn't go fast, but we didn't mind. We were just glad to be outside playing.

Captain Juarez's voice came over my headset. "Stay close," he said. "There's something I want to show you."

We retraced our tracks back toward the dome. When we got to within about half a kilometer, we took a sharp right and skirted the base of a large hill. I eased us through a pothole, then glanced up and immediately slammed on the brakes.

Before us was a dome just like the one we lived in. But it was smaller and it looked completely finished, like someone could move right in.

"What is it?" Natasha asked.

"It's the base station," Captain Juarez answered. "It's where the workers lived until the big dome was built."

He took us inside. The building had a kitchen, a bathroom, and about 10 sleeping cubicles. All in all, it was a miniature version of the big dome.

"I didn't know there was already a building on the moon," Suzca said, as we looked around the place.

"That's because nobody wanted you or anyone else to know," the captain said.

"Why not?" Jerry asked.

"There's a lot of publicity about the Moon Colony," the captain said. "I think the powers-that-be thought it would take away from the project if the public realized that there was already a building on the moon."

"Why are you showing it to us now?" Harry asked.

"Because I was thinking that with all the construction going on in the big dome, this might be a good place to conduct school. It's still stocked with food and water. We have everything we need right here. And I wanted to show it to you guys—get your opinions—before I asked the major for permission."

Before anyone could respond, we heard the crackle of the radio in the rover. "Stay here," the captain ordered.

We watched as he talked over the radio. It wasn't connected to our headsets so we couldn't hear a thing. But we saw him frown deeply. When he came back into the dome, it was obvious to all of us that he was upset.

"What's going on?" I asked.

"It's time to leave," he said.

"You're not answering my question."

Sighing, he said, "Adam, I was told to get you back to the dome. So please do as I say, OK?" He moved toward the door, but none of us followed. The captain turned, irritated.

"What's the problem here?" he demanded.

"You want to know the problem?" I countered. "You were the only one who didn't treat us like kids."

"That's right," Natasha added. "You talked to us. You told us things."

"Come on, Captain Juarez," Suzca coaxed. "Don't start acting like our parents now. Tell us what's wrong. We have a right to know."

The captain paced back and forth, clearly torn. Finally, he said, "You're right. You do have a right to know." He took a deep breath. "The drought has hit Hadouth. They've asked Umbria for aid." He paused, then added, "Umbria said no."

Chapter Nine

Nothing was the same after that. We didn't sit around as a group anymore to listen to the news. Instead, each family monitored events on Earth from their own cubicle. And each set of parents talked by radio, in private, to their country's leaders.

By the end of the week, the Moon Colony had split into two camps. The Hadouthians and Danjans made up one group. The Loovers, Umbrians, and Grazians made up the other. We still ate together, but the silence was thicker than the gravy on our plates. And while the adults continued to work on the inner dome, we kids could often hear them bickering through the thin plastic.

Overall, there was a lot of whispering going on. A lot of conversations stopped abruptly when the wrong person walked into a room.

Strangely enough, the only thing that kept me sane was school. We were in different grades. So Captain Juarez broke us up into small groups. Then he would work with each group in turn. Suzca and Natasha were in my group. The captain didn't mind if we talked quietly while he taught the younger kids. And talking sure helped. I was beginning to know the girls pretty well. In some ways, I felt closer to them than I did to my friends at home.

"Did you hear what they said over the radio?" Natasha asked one day. It was a goal of ours—we were trying to overhear our parents' radio conversations. We figured that all the important stuff about Umbria and Hadouth—stuff that wasn't on the news—was being discussed by radio.

Suzca and I shook our heads. "Did you?" I asked.

"No," Natasha said in a disgusted voice. "And when I ask what's going on, they just tell me not to worry."

"Same here," Suzca said. "Although I did hear my parents talking last night about segregating us."

"Segregating us?" Natasha drew back. "What does that mean?"

"I think it means that they want to keep us apart," Suzca said.

"I think you're right," I added miserably.

"But why?" Natasha asked.

Suzca raised her shoulders hopelessly. "Because our countries disagree about helping each other, I guess."

Natasha bit her lip. I could see tears in her eyes. "You guys are the only good thing about this place," she said.

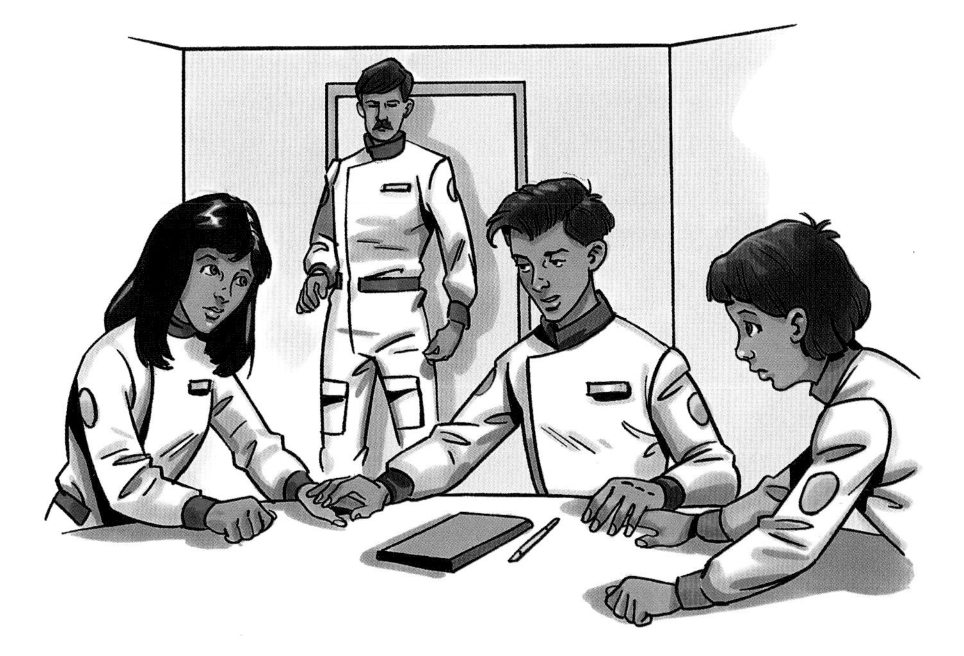

Then she raised her head and the tears were gone, replaced by steely determination. “I’m not mad at you. And I promise,” she said, holding out her hand, “that I never will be.”

I put my hand on her hand.

“I promise,” I said.

“Me, too,” Suzca said.

“So do I,” a fourth voice said.

We glanced up to see Captain Juarez standing over us. “I’m not sure what I just promised,” he said. “But could we unlink our hands long enough to open our books? It’s time for the most fun lesson . . .”

"Algebra," we all groaned together.

That night, I decided enough was enough. I was going to talk to my parents like Captain Juarez had suggested on the first day of school. I went in their cubicle and sat on my mom's cot. She was propped up on her pillows, working on her laptop. My dad was lying on the opposite cot, reading a book.

"Can I talk to you guys?" I asked.

"Always, honey," my mom said as she shut off the computer.

My knee started to bounce nervously. Now that I had their attention, I didn't know what to say. No, that's not right—I knew what I had to say. But I didn't know *how* to say it. How do you tell your parents that they're acting like kids? How exactly do you phrase that without making things worse?

"Is something bothering you, son?" my dad asked.

He looked really worried. And it struck me then—he cares so much. He and all the other parents in the colony would do anything for their kids. They were nice people. And that kind of made it more confusing for me. To me, there were no bad guys here. There was no one you could point a finger at and say, "It's his or her fault." Instead, we had a bunch of good people who weren't acting like themselves.

"Adam?" my dad prompted. "Is there something you want to say?"

I nodded.

"Well then, speak up, son. It's nearly time for bed."

I swallowed hard. It's now or never, I thought. "It's like this," I said aloud. "We're hearing rumors that you adults are thinking about keeping us kids apart. And we just wanted you to know that . . ."

"Where did you hear that?" my dad interrupted, frowning.

I hesitated—I didn't want to get Suzca in trouble. "Does it matter?" I asked at last.

"Yes. Yes, it does." My dad sat up and put his legs over the side of the bed so that we were facing one another. "Rumors can be dangerous," he said, "especially at a time like this. I'd like to know who's starting them so that I can put a stop to it immediately."

I sighed in exasperation. "You know, if you would tell us what's going on, we wouldn't be spreading rumors."

"What exactly do you want to hear, son? You listen to the news every day."

"And you talk on the radio every night," I countered. "We don't know what you're saying—none of you will tell us. And that makes it worse. That makes us think of all kinds of scary things. Don't you see? Keeping quiet is scaring us."

My dad started to argue, but my mom raised her hand. "Wait a minute," she said. "He's right."

She moved to my side and put an arm around me.

"Adam, the radio conversations basically deal with keeping the lines of supply open. Every week, a different country was scheduled to send supplies to the moon. If, because of the drought, one country does not send its weekly shipment, then we have to be prepared."

"That's it?" I asked dubiously.

Both she and my dad nodded.

"Well then, why all the secrecy?"

"If we have to step in and send an unscheduled shipment, we want to be sure no one interferes with it," my mom explained.

"You mean, like the Hadouthians?"

She shrugged vaguely.

I thought this over. Then I shook my head. "That doesn't make sense. Why would the Hadouthians stop a shipment? They have a family up here, too."

Sighing, she said, "I really don't know if they would or not. I just know that we have to be prepared."

I started to ask more questions—like how they planned to stop someone from interfering with the shipment—but my dad reached over to pat my leg.

"There. Now you know what we say over the radio. Better?" He sat back and picked up his book like everything was fine.

"Dad?"

He glanced up. "Yes?"

"Are you really going to keep us kids apart?"

He rolled his eyes and lowered his book. "Adam, if

we feel it's for the best, then yes, we'll separate . . ."

"How can you say it's for the best? You haven't asked us, have you?"

He raised his hands in the air, then let them drop in his lap like he always does when he's irritated. "Why does this matter to you so much?"

"Because . . . because . . ." I couldn't find the words. Then I remembered what Natasha had said earlier. "Because the kids are the only good thing about being here."

"Oh, Adam." My mom tried to hug me.

But I pushed her away and stood up. "You said once that you respected my opinion," I told my dad. "Well, here it is: The day we left for the moon, everyone was saying how this was such a great example of cooperation among nations. Maybe you've forgotten that. But I haven't. And it might be OK with you that we're all suddenly supposed to be mad at each other. But I don't like it. So don't try to take away my friends. Right now, I'd rather be with them than you."

I stomped out of their room and into mine. I could hear my parents speaking in low voices. I could tell my mom was upset. But I just rolled over and put the pillow over my head. I stayed that way for a long time. Lights went out one by one. The whole dome was quiet. Then I felt someone tugging on my sleeve.

It was Natasha. I could barely make her out in the dark. I started to say something, but she raised a finger to her lips.

"Shhh," she whispered. "We'll get in trouble if they find us." Then she beckoned me to follow. We tiptoed down the hall, past the sleeping quarters, to the kitchen.

"What's wrong?" I asked her once we were out of earshot of anyone who might still be awake.

"Did you hear me fighting with my parents?"

I smiled dryly. "No. I was too busy fighting with mine."

"Well, it's true. They are planning to separate us."

"Yeah, I know. That's the impression I got, too."

She took my hand. "Adam, we can't let that happen."

"No," I agreed. "We can't."

"Good. I'm glad you feel that way. Because I think I know how to stop them."

Chapter Ten

Every morning at school, we had a snack break around ten o'clock. The break was more for Captain Juarez's benefit than ours. Since he was also the cook for the colony, the 30-minute break gave him time to prepare for lunch. While we ate our fruit, he was usually busy in the kitchen, slicing homemade bread or tossing a salad. It was a perfect time for Natasha and me to tell Suzca about our plan. We were huddled together at the end of the table, whispering back and forth.

"It's a great idea!" Suzca said when we had finished.

Her voice came out loud. The three of us immediately glanced at the younger kids. They were gazing at the ceiling or down at the floor, pretending not to listen. But they weren't talking among themselves and it was obvious that they were straining to hear every word we said. I felt sort of sorry for them. The adults had closed them out, and now we were, too. "What should we do about them?" Suzca whispered, jerking her head toward the other kids.

"I don't know," I said. "It could be dangerous. I'm not sure if we should take them along. What do you think, Natasha?"

"I'm not sure, either," she said slowly. "I think I agree with you, Adam, but . . ." She looked to Suzca. "Neither Adam nor I have siblings. You have Kyle and Joss. So maybe you should make the call."

Suzca bit her lip, thinking it over. Finally, she said, "I hate to leave them behind, but if something should happen to them . . ." She trailed off.

In my mind I pictured one of the little kids crying—or worse, injured. "I think they should stay," I said. To my relief, both girls nodded.

With that settled, we moved on to other business. "When do we do it?" Suzca asked.

"How about tonight?" I offered.

"That's good," Natasha said. "We should wait until about two o'clock. That way, everyone should be asleep. Remember, we have to be very . . ."

"Quiet!" I hissed.

"Huh?" Natasha looked at me blankly.

I nodded toward the kitchen. Captain Juarez was leaning against the doorway with his arms folded across his chest. He looked relaxed, but his eyes were like an eagle's, watching our every move. He pushed away from the door and came over to stand by us.

"What's up?" he asked lightly.

"Nothing," I said—too quickly, I thought. I sounded guilty even to my own ears.

"Really?" The captain raised his eyebrows skeptically. "You wouldn't lie to me, would you, Adam?"

I swallowed hard. My mouth moved silently. Natasha came to my rescue.

"We were just talking about our parents—how we don't like how they're acting," she explained.

"Did you tell them that?" the captain asked.

All three of us nodded.

"What did they say?"

None of us spoke. We just stared at the table. Finally, Suzca said, "It didn't help."

The captain gave a sigh and turned away for a moment. When he looked back at us, he said, "I know you guys are frustrated. So am I. And believe it or not, so are your parents. They don't like this situation any better than you."

"But they're causing this situation," Natasha pointed out.

"No," the captain said firmly. "The drought is causing this situation. Your parents are trying to deal with it as best they can."

"You really think they're doing the best they can?" I asked.

The captain hesitated—it was clear that he had his doubts, too. Finally, he said, "I think they need time to adjust. And when they do . . . well, things will get better. OK?"

No one answered. The captain sighed.

"I know it's hard," he said. "But I want you guys to promise me that you won't do anything rash. Just . . . just give them some time to come around before you do something you might regret. Will you promise me that?"

I looked at the girls in turn. In their eyes, I saw the same mixed emotions that I felt—none of us wanted to lie to the captain. We liked him. He'd always been honest with us. But if we told him the truth, our plan was sunk.

"I promise," I said woodenly.

"Me, too," Natasha echoed.

Suzca closed her eyes briefly. "OK," she said. "I promise."

That night when two o'clock rolled around, we all broke our promise.

I slid out of bed and dressed in the dark. I could hear the muffled movements of Natasha across the hall. I picked up my pack and we crept toward the kitchen. Suzca joined us halfway there. Without a

word, Natasha placed a slip of paper on the kitchen table. Then we entered the containment room to put on our space suits.

I really don't know how they figured it out, but all the other kids were waiting for us in the containment room. They were already suited up, except for their helmets, and their eyes were shining defiantly.

"What are you doing here?" Suzca demanded.

Her little brother Kyle spoke up. "We took a vote. And we're coming, too."

"But you can't," I protested. "It's too dangerous."

"If you won't let us go," Harry said calmly, "then we'll wake up all the adults."

Natasha, Suzca, and I looked at one another. The same thoughts were racing through our minds. We didn't have time to argue with these kids. And we certainly didn't want our parents to wake up.

What could we do? We had no choice but to take them.

"All right," I said wearily. "Let's get moving."

After we were all suited up and our helmets securely fastened, I led the way out to the lunar rover. There were nine of us now, but with the little ones sitting on the bigger ones' laps, we managed to squeeze everyone in.

"All set?" I asked as I climbed in the driver's seat.

I got eight thumbs up signs. I pushed the start button and shifted gears. As we rolled forward, I glanced at Natasha. She was smiling. So was I.

There was no turning back now.

It took about 20 minutes to get to the base station. I drove slowly over the rocks, thinking that the last thing we needed was an accident.

As soon as the rover stopped, we all tumbled out. Little Lee was nearly asleep so I carried her to the door. We stripped off our suits in the containment room. Once inside, Natasha hit the lights. While I lowered Lee into the nearest chair, Natasha and Suzca began rummaging through the kitchen cupboards.

"What's the verdict?" I asked. "Was the captain right? Do we have food and water?"

Suzca turned, holding up a can of soup. "Well, it's not home cooking, but it'll do," she said, grinning.

"We're set," Natasha added as she twisted the cap off a bottle of water. "We could stay here for months."

"Months?" Harry asked in a small voice.

I scanned the faces of the younger ones. Back at the dome, they had looked brave. Now they were tired and more importantly, just now realizing that their mommies and daddies weren't around. I had scared kids on my hands and I had to do something fast.

"Please sit down," I told them, gesturing to the table.

When everyone was seated, I took a deep breath and said, "As you all know, our parents are fighting. They're acting like we're all enemies or something. So we—that is, Natasha, Suzca, and I—have decided to do something about it. We came up with this plan. And you guys insisted upon coming along."

I paused and looked at each of them in turn. "By now, some of you may have changed your minds. That's understandable. When I was your age, I didn't like to be away from my parents, either. So here's the deal—if anyone wants to go back to the dome, I'll take them. But it has to be now. I can't do it later."

Jerry shifted in his seat. "How long are we going to be here?" he asked.

"I don't know," I answered honestly.

"As long as it takes," Natasha put in.

Saul raised his hand. "You said you couldn't take us back later?"

"That's right," Suzca said.

"Why not?" he asked.

"Because the plan won't work if anyone leaves," I explained. "We have to present a united front. They can't think they can break us."

In the silence that followed, Natasha leaned forward and folded her arms on the table. "OK. You understand our position. Now it's time for a decision. Who wants to go back to the dome?"

The kids looked at one another, but they all kept quiet.

"Don't be embarrassed," Suzca said gently. "If you want to go, we'll understand. No one will make fun of you."

Again, the kids exchanged glances. Harry was the first to speak.

"I want to stay," he said.

"Me, too," Jerry echoed.

"So do I," Saul said.

Suzca's siblings nodded their agreement. Everyone was in, except for little Lee. I reached over and put her on my lap. "What about you?" I asked. "Do you want to stay or go?"

She rubbed her eyes sleepily. "Which one is my bed?" she asked.

Chapter Eleven

Captain Juarez made breakfast every day, so he was up before anyone else. We found out later that he was the first to find the letter we left on the kitchen table. As he read it, his face turned pale. He half started toward the door. Then he thought better and went dashing down the hall.

"Wake up! Wake up!" he shouted.

Our parents came awake instantly. Disaster was on their minds, so they were prepared, in a way, for an uproar at the break of dawn. In their robes and their slippers, they ran out into the hall. Imagine their surprise when they heard the captain's news.

"All the children are gone," he said. He was gasping for breath as though he had run a mile.

"Gone?" my father repeated. He wasn't sure he had heard right. "What do you mean, they're gone?"

"They left this," the captain said, waving the paper in his hand. "This letter explains everything."

"Let me see that," Natasha's dad said. He snatched the letter and his lips moved silently as he read.

"Read it aloud!" Dr. Wingee exclaimed.

Placker dutifully read the letter out loud. It said:

To Whom It May Concern:

We, the children of the Moon Colony, have a major problem with the way things are going. We do not think it is necessary to act like enemies. In fact, we think it is wrong. And we refuse to treat our friends badly, whether they live on Earth or on the moon.

Our parents, however, have been fighting since the drought escalated. Their attitude concerns us. We believe it will lead to bigger problems down the road. Also, we believe that such fighting is contrary to the stated mission of the Moon Colony, which was to set an example for cooperation among nations. That, at least, is what we were told.

For these reasons, we are leaving the dome and forming our own colony. We will live in the base station. We have plenty of food and water so there's no need to worry about us.

We have decided to rename the base station. It will now be called the Peace Colony. No one is allowed to enter unless they are friendly. We are willing to discuss our move with our parents. However, we are not willing to return to the big dome unless major changes are made.

Signed,

The Children of the Peace Colony

"What in the world were they thinking?" my mom asked in a faint voice.

My dad quickly helped her down the hall to a chair. The rest of the group followed, including Captain Juarez and Major Hinley. Most were dazed. But some, like Lee and Saul's mother, were frantic.

"They took my babies?" she was saying. "They took my little babies?"

"What do you mean, 'they'?" Suzca's dad asked irritably.

"Well, the oldest kids, of course," she answered. "My Saul is only ten and Lee just turned seven. They didn't come up with this silly plan."

"Don't try to blame this on my daughter," he snapped. "Suzca's a good girl."

"No one's trying to blame anyone," Natasha's mom said soothingly.

But Suzca's mom countered, "That's easy for you to say. Your daughter is 14. But my Kyle and Joss . . . they're too young to be out there all alone."

"They're all too young to be out there alone," my dad said grimly.

Natasha's dad looked at mine and said, "I bet your boy started this whole . . ."

"Stop!"

Everyone turned at the sound of Captain Juarez's voice. He was standing at the head of the table with his hands on his hips. In an angry tone, he said, "Would you listen to yourselves? Your kids just ran away because they couldn't stand your bickering. And how do you react? You bicker!" He paused and shook his head sadly. "I don't have kids," he said. "But if I did and they pulled something like this . . . well, I think it would make me take a hard look at myself. I think I'd be trying to figure out how to get them back instead of placing the blame on someone else."

"Captain Juarez!" Major Hinley said in a shocked voice. "You will apologize to these people."

"No," my mom said quietly.

Everyone turned toward her.

"Don't you see—he's right," she continued. "We've been acting like fools. I, for one, am deeply ashamed of my behavior. And I intend to do something about it. But first, I want to thank the captain for his wise words."

"You're welcome," the captain said, smiling.

"Now," my mother said, standing up. "Captain, I need one more favor from you."

He spread his hands wide. "I'm here to help," he said.

"Excellent. Then would you kindly direct me to the base station? I owe someone there an apology."

Back at the base station, or Peace Colony as we liked to call it, we were waking up one by one. Harry and Jerry were the earliest risers. They had already mixed some dry milk with water and were eating cereal by the time Suzca got up. When I finally stumbled down the hall, everyone was sitting around the table, picking half-heartedly at their breakfast. We had all gone to bed late. None of us had gotten a good night's sleep, and the little kids in particular looked beat.

"How's everyone feeling this morning?" I asked, trying to sound cheerful.

Natasha glanced up from her mug of tea and smiled. "Fine," she answered.

She was, in fact, the only one who did look fine. On closer inspection, I saw that the little ones weren't tired—they were sad. Even Suzca was down. She was obviously worried about her little brothers. As I poured myself some milk, I noticed that Joss was whispering to her. I heard something about "missing Mom" as I walked past their chairs. I started to sit, but Suzca gestured to Natasha and me.

We followed her down the hall. When we were out of earshot of the little ones, she said, "I think we have a problem."

"What's up?" I asked.

"Well, the little kids have been talking to me. And they all want to go home."

Natasha frowned. "But last night they agreed to stay."

"That was last night," Suzca said. "This morning they woke up and there's no mom or dad. . . .You have to understand, they're just little. They mean well, but I don't think they're going to last another night."

"What should we do?" Natasha asked.

I shrugged helplessly. "Take them back, I guess."

"But we said we weren't going to do that," she protested.

"I know, but we can't force them to stay."

Suzca agreed with me. "If we did that, we'd be acting as bad as our parents," she pointed out.

"You're right," Natasha conceded. She started to add more, but Joss gave a shout:

"Someone's coming!"

We all ran to the door. We could see lunar rovers pulling up outside.

Our parents were here.

"Mommy!" Lee squealed, obviously delighted.

I picked her up and sat her down in a chair. "Everybody come here," I directed.

When they were all settled around the table, I said, "Listen to me closely: our parents have come here to take us back. If we run right to them, they'll think everything's fine and nothing will change. I know you all want to go home. But I'm asking you to stay tough for a few minutes longer. Give me a chance to talk to them. Give me one chance to convince them to quit fighting. If I fail and you still want to go with them, you can. I'm just asking for a few minutes, OK?"

To my surprise, every one of them agreed. "We'll just sit here quietly," Kyle promised solemnly.

By this time, our parents were in the containment room, taking off their space suits. Natasha, Suzca, and I were waiting for them as they entered the Peace Colony. Their eyes were downcast. They looked like we kids look when we've done something wrong—sorry and willing to please.

Before we said a word, my mother walked up to us and handed us a letter. Puzzled, I read it aloud:

To the Children of the Peace Colony:

We, the parents of the Moon Colony, are here to apologize for our shameful behavior. We realize that we were wrong. And we promise to quit fighting. We are asking you to give us another chance. Please come home. We miss you and we love you.

Signed,

The Parents of the Moon Colony

I looked up from the letter, grinning broadly. "We won!" I shouted.

And we all ran into the arms of our parents.

We only won a small victory. Things on Earth haven't changed. Every day, we get reports about which country is mad at the other. But here, at the Moon Colony, we're doing our best to make sure that in one little part of this universe, peace reigns.